Hoofbeats

THE STORY OF A THOROUGHBRED

Cynthia McFarland

ATHENEUM   1993   New York

MAXWELL MACMILLAN CANADA   MAXWELL MACMILLAN INTERNATIONAL

Atheneum
Macmillan Publishing Company
866 Third Avenue
New York, NY 10022

Maxwell Macmillan Canada, Inc.
1200 Eglinton Avenue East
Suite 200
Don Mills, Ontario M3C 3N1

Macmillan Publishing Company is part of the
Maxwell Communication Group of Companies.

First edition
Printed in the United States of America
10 9 8 7 6 5 4 3 2 1
The text of this book is set in Cochin.
Book design by Black Angus Design Group

Library of Congress Cataloging-in-Publication Data

McFarland, Cynthia.
Hoofbeats: the story of a Thoroughbred / by Cynthia McFarland.—
1st. ed.
p.   cm.
Summary: Text and photographs describe the life of a Thoroughbred
racehorse, from birth through training to its first race as a two-
year-old.
ISBN 0–689–31757–3
1. Thoroughbred horse—Juvenile literature.   2. Racehorses—
Juvenile literature.   [1. Thoroughbred horse.   2. Racehorses.
3. Horse racing.]   I. Title.
SF293.T5M44 1993
636.1′32—dc20   92–14255

With much appreciation to BryLynn Farm, Blackthorn Farm,
Quail Roost Farm, and Bonnie Heath Farm;
also to Melvin James for sharing his time
and expertise regarding training.
A heartfelt thank-you to those friends and family
whose support is a continual encouragement;
and to Yuma and Sierra, the horses in my life,
who bring much joy.

At Silver Meadows Farm there are horses grazing on the rolling green hills. There are horses dozing in the shade of the tall oak trees, and there are horses in the stalls of the big white barns. Early in the morning, when mist swirls across the pastures, there is the sound of hoofbeats in the still air as horses gallop around the training track.

The horses at Silver Meadows are Thoroughbreds. For nearly three hundred years the Thoroughbred has been carefully bred to be a racehorse with the strength and endurance to run faster and farther than any other animal in the world. His long, powerful legs can carry him a mile in as little as one minute and thirty-five seconds, at a speed up to forty-five miles per hour. Running is simply what the Thoroughbred does best.

A mare is an adult female horse. A broodmare is a mare used for breeding to produce offspring called foals. When an owner chooses a male horse, or stallion, to breed with his mare, he looks for many things. He needs to know the horse's race record and its family history, or pedigree. It is important for the stallion and broodmare to have good builds, or conformation, to pass on to their foal.

Thousands of foals are born every year, but not all will be good enough to race. A foal with nice conformation and pedigree usually has a better chance of being a racehorse.

Broodmares spend their days in the pasture. The sun warms their bright coats as they eat the lush grass. The broodmares will carry their unborn foals for about 335 days, or 11 months. When the time for foaling draws close, Bob, the farm manager, will keep them in the barn where he can watch to be sure their foals are born safely.

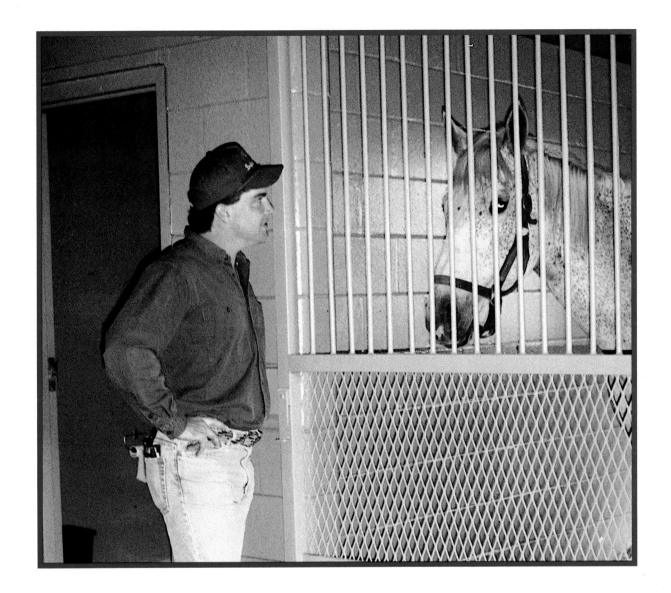

Tonight the big gray mare in the first stall is restless. She hasn't finished eating her grain. When Bob checks her later in the evening, she is pacing the stall. Bob calls her name and the mare flicks an ear toward him, then stomps a hind foot. Her shoulders are damp with sweat.

The gray mare knows. Bob knows. It will be soon.

Very early in the morning, before the sun's first light colors the sky, a Thoroughbred is born. Bob works closely with the mare as she delivers her foal. He makes sure the baby's nose and mouth are clear of mucus so it can breathe easily.

A male foal is called a colt. A female foal is a filly. The gray mare has had a colt.

The gray mare is tired. Bob gently pulls the dark, slippery foal around to the mare's head so she can meet her new baby while she rests in the hay.

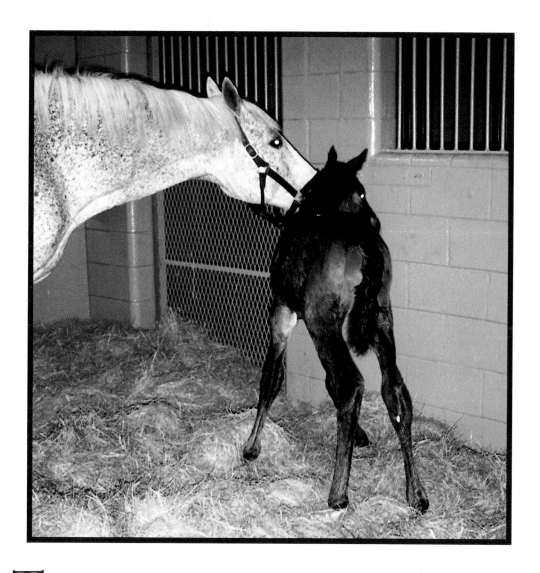

The mare nuzzles her new colt, sniffing and licking his wet coat. She is careful not to step on him when she gets to her feet.

The gray mare gives a low whinny and the baby answers with a shrill nicker. Soon he tries to stand, but his long legs get in the way. Bob helps steady the newborn foal, who learns to take clumsy, wobbling steps in less than an hour. The foal will be able to run the same day it is born.

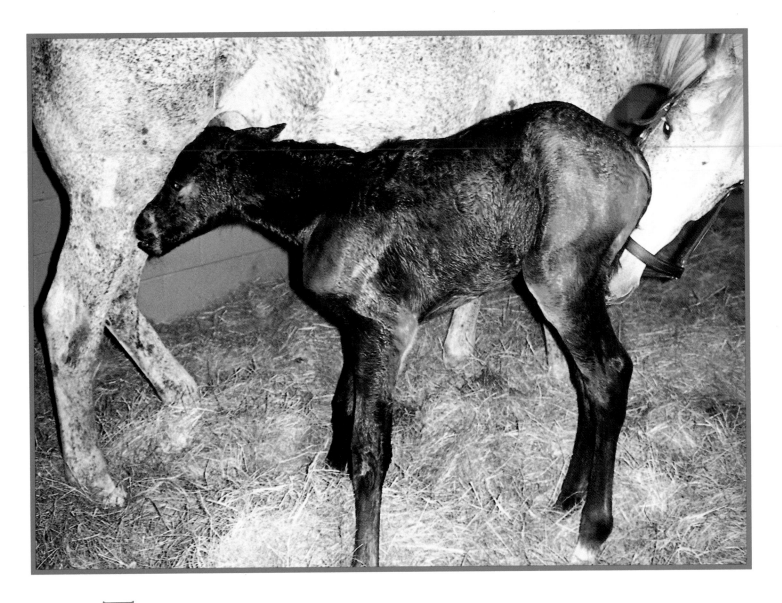

The mare stands quietly as her foal finds his meal. Her first milk is called colostrum and has important nutrients to protect the new baby from diseases.

After the foal nurses he is soon fast asleep. Later that morning the veterinarian stops by the farm. He gives the foal a shot and takes a blood sample that will be tested to make sure the colt is healthy.

The colt and his mother spend the first few days of his life in their own paddock. When he isn't sleeping in the grass, the colt stays close to his mother's side.

A foal is born without teeth. The first teeth begin to grow in within a week. Though he gets all the nourishment he needs from his mother's milk, the colt soon learns to eat grass. When the gray mare eats her grain each day, her colt nibbles at the feed.

Soon the colt and his mother are turned out into a larger pasture with other broodmares and young foals. The foals like to play together. If the weather is nice, the horses sleep outside at night, but if it is cold or rainy, Bob will bring them into the barn.

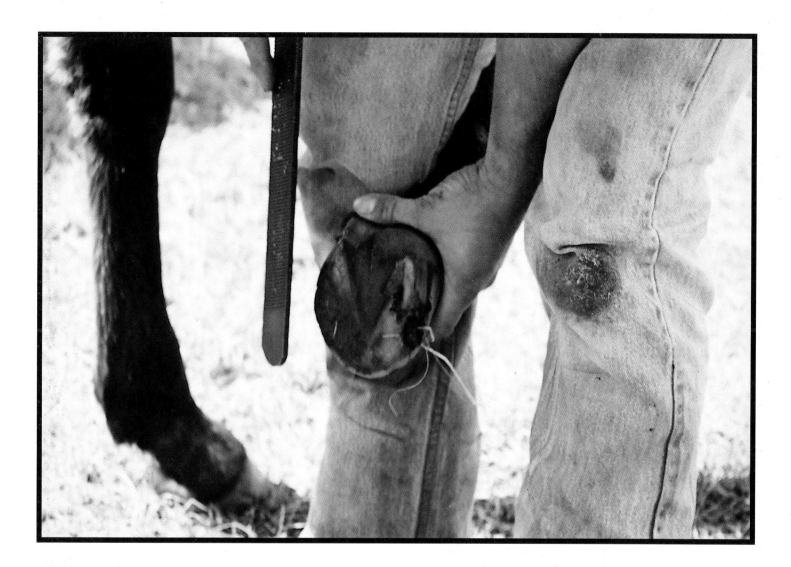

Every six weeks the blacksmith trims the horses' hooves. A hoof is not made of bone but is like a very hard fingernail, so having his hooves trimmed doesn't hurt the colt. The blacksmith cuts away the extra that has grown and files the edges smooth. When the colt's hooves are kept trimmed and even, it is more likely that the animal's legs will grow straight. When the colt is older, the blacksmith will nail horseshoes to his hooves.

Spring and summer pass, and the gray mare's colt grows much taller and heavier, finally growing into the long legs he was born with.

Jenny is one of the grooms at the farm. Every morning Jenny grooms the broodmares and foals, brushing until their coats are slick and clean. The color of the foals' coats often changes as they grow older and shed their fuzzy baby hair. The colt likes the feel of the brush on his back. His coat is warm and smooth as velvet.

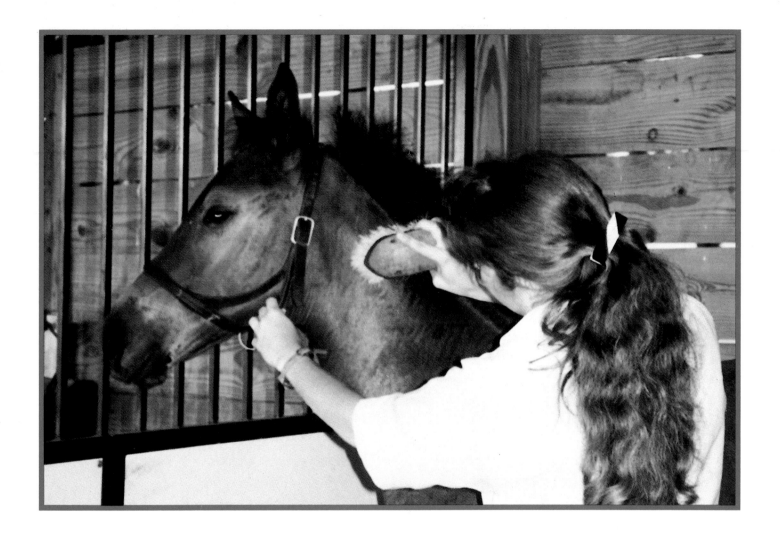

The colt wears a soft leather halter on his head. After he is groomed, Jenny leads the colt with a rope hooked to his halter, teaching him to follow and obey.

By the time the foals are about six months old, they are ready to be weaned from their mothers. They are eating grass, hay, and grain, and no longer need to nurse. Their mothers have already been bred again and are pregnant with the foals that will be born next spring.

The mares are taken to another field where they can't see or hear their foals. Now called weanlings, the foals are soon accustomed to being apart from their mothers and play together.

The gray mare's colt has been named Sailed at Dawn, but Jenny and the other grooms call him Sailor.

Whether foals are born in winter or late spring, all Thorough-breds celebrate their birthday on the first day of January each year.

For most of their yearling—or first—year, Sailor and the other colts spend their days eating, playing, and growing. One day they may meet on the racetrack, but now they gallop across the field just for fun. The rich grass they eat helps their bones grow strong. Grain and hay provide nutrition they need to develop into adult horses.

Bred and raised to be a racehorse, Sailor will go into training just before he turns two.

Mel James is the trainer at Silver Meadows Farm. Mel looks over each yearling and decides if it is ready to begin training. Those that need to grow bigger and stronger will not start training until they are two-year-olds. The yearlings that are ready are moved to the farm's training barn.

Before he learns to carry a rider on his back, Sailor must get used to the saddle and bridle. The bridle has a metal bit that goes in the colt's mouth. Reins are attached to the bit to guide the colt. Sailor chomps and chews on the strange thing in his mouth, but soon he accepts the bit.

The saddle weighs only about five pounds and is held on the colt's back by the girth, which goes around his belly.

Carol is the exercise rider who will begin riding Sailor. Once he is comfortable with the saddle and bridle, Carol sits on his back. She asks him to turn in both directions by gently pulling on the bridle reins. After he learns to obey, Sailor is taken outside to a small paddock. At first they only walk and trot around the paddock. When it is clear that the colt understands Carol's commands, she will ask him to canter. After several weeks Sailor is ready to go to the training track.

Mel sends Sailor to the track with another young horse each morning. They walk and jog around the track. When he feels Sailor is ready, Mel will have the rider begin galloping the colt. Young horses gallop about one quarter of a mile each day and work up to almost a mile a day. They do not yet run at racing speed, but they are getting stronger and more fit. As Sailor improves, the trainer will work him with different horses so that he learns to be competitive.

Even if he is galloping well, Sailor can't be entered in a race until he learns one of his most important lessons: the starting gate. At first the exercise rider only walks the colt through the gate. After Sailor is comfortable with this, the trainer will shut the doors, closing the colt in. He wants the colt to be alert, to look ahead, and to stand evenly so he can start quickly when the gate opens. Once Sailor has learned to stand and start from the gate, he is almost ready to race. About five months have passed since Sailor began training.

Ready for his first real race, Sailor travels to the racetrack in a large horse van. A groom from the training barn travels with him.

There are many different sights and sounds at the track. From his stall Sailor can see the other horses and their trainers, riders, grooms, and veterinarians come and go throughout the day. He hears the bugle call horses to the track, and the clang of the starter's bell as a race begins. He listens to the noise of the crowd as they cheer and clap, and to the muffled thunder of hoofbeats as horses race around the turn and down the homestretch.

The jockey is the person the horse's owner hires to ride the horse in a race. The trainer talks with the jockey before the race and may give him special instructions about the horse.

At the call "Riders up!" the jockeys mount. As the racehorses walk out to the track, a lead, or pony, horse goes beside Sailor as he warms up. A pony horse is solid, quiet, and dependable. The pony horse helps the young racehorse stay calm. His rider can help the jockey if Sailor acts skittish or frightened before the race and as they load into the starting gate.

The horses reach the starting gate. As soon as the last horse is loaded, the bell sounds and the horses burst from the gate and race down the track. The jockeys ride low on their horses' backs during the race.

When they cross the wire, or finish line, Sailor is in second place. After the finish the jockeys stand up in their saddles and slow their horses down.

A groom takes Sailor from the jockey after the race and walks the colt back to the barn, where the trainer will meet them. Mel is pleased with Sailor's effort. Because the colt ran so well in his first race, the trainer feels he will have a good chance of winning his next start.

Grooms bathe Sailor, washing off the sweat and dirt from the track. The tired colt is walked until he is cool and dry, then turned into his freshly bedded stall.

Many miles away, back at Silver Meadows Farm, there is no cheering from a crowded grandstand, no bugle calling sleek, prancing Thoroughbreds to the post.

There is only the gentle whisper of a breeze in the tall oaks and the sound of horses cropping grass as they graze peacefully. There is the swish of a tail and the whinny of a mare calling to her foal.

And in the pasture near the broodmare barn, a gray mare, Sailor's mother, is grazing quietly while a new, wobbly-legged foal rests close at her side.

GLOSSARY

bit. metal mouthpiece on a bridle to which reins are attached to control the horse.

blacksmith. someone whose occupation involves working with iron, making and fitting horseshoes; sometimes referred to as a farrier.

bridle. head harness for a horse that allows a rider to control him or her.

broodmare. adult female horse used for breeding to produce offspring, called foals.

canter. a smooth, three-beat gait like a slow gallop.

colostrum. the first milk produced by the new mother after having given birth, very rich in protein.

colt. a male foal or young male horse.

conformation. the shape or build of an animal.

filly. a female foal or young female horse.

foal. a baby horse of either sex.

gallop. the horse's fastest, three-beat gait.

girth. band of leather or strong cloth that fits around the horse's belly to hold the saddle in place.

groom. someone who cares for horses, doing such chores as feeding and brushing.

halter. headpiece for a horse without bit or reins, to which a rope can be attached to lead or tie the horse.

homestretch. final straight distance in the race before the finish line.

horseshoe. metal formed by the blacksmith to be nailed to bottom edge of a horse's hoof for protection.

jockey. professional rider who rides a horse in a race.

jog. slow trot, a two-beat gait.

load. to put a horse into a horse trailer for transportation; also to move a horse into the starting gate.

mare. an adult female horse at least five years old that may be used for breeding.

nicker. a low, whinnying sound made by a horse.

paddock. a small fenced area where a horse can be ridden or turned out for exercise.

pedigree. the bloodlines of a horse, the history of its relatives.

pony horse. a horse used to pony, or lead, a racehorse onto the track before the race. Can be any breed of horse but must be quiet, dependable, responsive, and not easily upset.

reins. the parts of the bridle attached to the bit that the rider holds to control and guide the horse.

saddle. padded leather seat where the rider sits on the horse's back.

stallion. an adult male horse that may be used for breeding.

starting gate. moveable metal unit with individual compartments, each having a front and back gate where a horse stands to start the race.

Thoroughbred. a breed of racehorse originally bred by crossing British mares with Arabian stallions.

trainer. a man or woman who supervises the horse's learning, or training.

trot. a horse's two-beat gait in which the horse's legs move forward in alternating diagonal pairs; slower than a canter.

veterinarian. a doctor who treats animals.

walk. the horse's slowest gait.

wean. to separate the mare from her foal when the foal doesn't need to nurse anymore, at about four to six months old.

weanling. a foal that has been weaned from his or her mother.

whinny. a sound a horse makes; resembles a neigh, a horse's loud cry.

wire. finish line in the race.

yearling. a young horse that is a year old.